TOOT TOOT

To Ellen and Amelia,
who went over the mountain with me,
and to Amy, a true friend
P. R.

For Janice
M. C.

Text copyright © 2009 by Phyllis Root
Illustrations copyright © 2009 by Matthew Cordell

First edition 2009

Library of Congress Cataloging-in-Publication Data is available.
Library of Congress Catalog Card Number 2008934781

ISBN 978-0-7636-3452-0

2 4 6 8 10 9 7 5 3

Printed in China

This book was typeset in Usherwood Medium.
The illustrations were done in ink and watercolor.

Candlewick Press
99 Dover Street
Somerville, Massachusetts 02144

visit us at www.candlewick.com

ZOOM!

Phyllis Root

illustrated by
Matthew Cordell

CANDLEWICK PRESS

POOR PIERRE!

He lived all alone at the foot of a sky-high mountain, and ah, his heart, how it longed for a friend.

"Perhaps," said Pierre, "I could find a friend on the other side of the mountain."

So Pierre hopped into his little red car, and off he zoomed to find a friend.

Up and up the road he zoomed.

At every curve he honked his horn.

Toot! Toot! Zoom!

Toot! Toot! Zoom!

TOOT! TOOT! TOOT! ZOOM!

TOOT!

TOOT!

"Where are you going so *toot-toot-zoom*?" bleated Goat in the middle of the road.

"Over the mountain to find a friend," said Pierre.

"I've always wanted to ride in a little red car," said Goat. "May I come, too, and help you find a friend?"

"That is exactly what my friend will ask, when I find a friend," said Pierre. "Hop in."

So Goat hopped in, and off they zoomed, Goat and Pierre, up and up the mountain.

Toot! Toot! Zoom!

"Where are you going so *toot-toot-zoom*?" baahed Sheep in the middle of the road.

"Over the mountain to find a friend," said Pierre.

"I've never been over the mountain," said Sheep. "May I come, too, and look for a friend?"

"Hop in," said Pierre.

So Sheep hopped in, and off they zoomed, Goat and Sheep and Pierre, over the mountain to find a friend.

"May I honk the horn?" asked Sheep.

"That is exactly what my friend will ask, when I find a friend!" cried Pierre.

Pierre let Sheep honk the horn.

Toot! Toot! Zoom!

Then Goat had a turn honking the horn.

Where are you going so *toot-toot-zoom*?" growled
Bear in the middle of the road.

"Over the mountain to find a friend," said Pierre.

"We're coming to help," said Goat and Sheep.

"A friend!" said Bear. "What a good thing to have.
May I come, too?"

"Hop in," said Pierre.

So Bear squeezed in, and off they zoomed,
Goat and Sheep and Bear and Pierre.

"Alas," cried Pierre, "my little car cannot make it over the mountain."

"Then we must push you!" growled Bear.

"That is exactly what my friend would do," said Pierre.

So Goat and Sheep and Bear all hopped out, and they pushed and they pushed the little red car . . .

to the very top of the mountain.

"Many thanks!" cried Pierre. "Hop in! Hop in!"

So Goat and Sheep and Bear hopped in, and off
they zoomed, down the other side of the mountain
to find Pierre a friend.

Toot! Toot! Zoom!

TooT! TOOT! ZOOM!

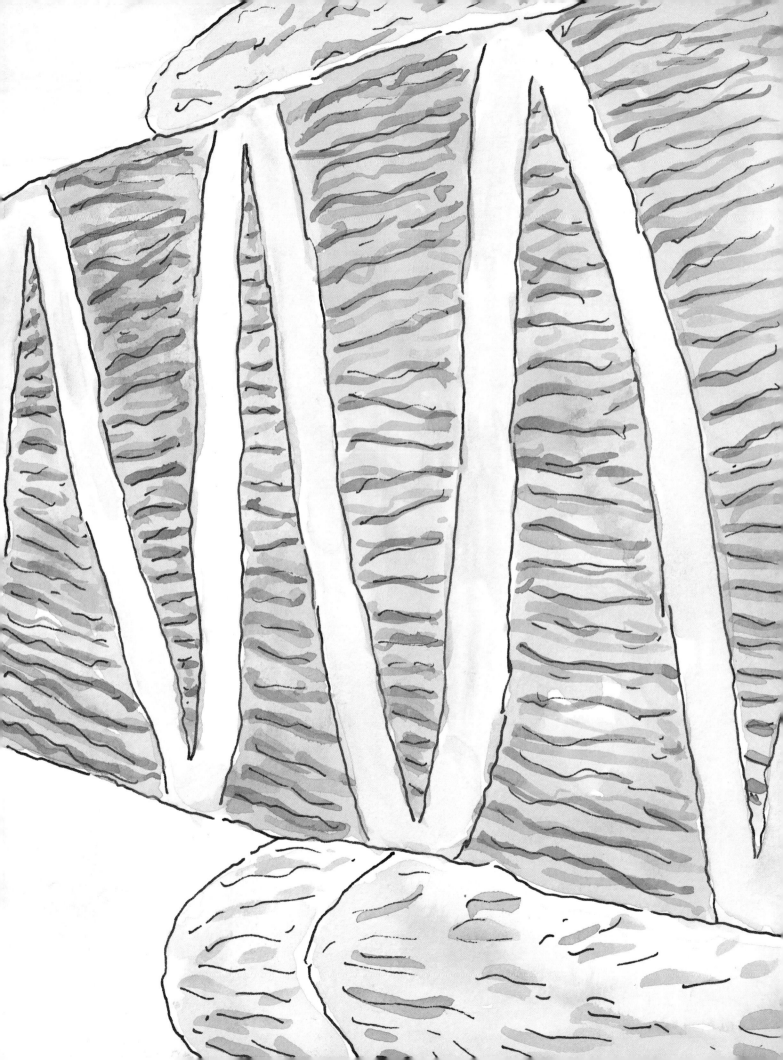

"Slow down!" screamed Goat and Sheep and Bear.

"No brakes!" cried Pierre.

"Is anyone hurt?" asked Pierre.

"Not I," bleated Goat.

"Not I," baahed Sheep.

"Not I," growled Bear.

"Not I," said Pierre.

But the little red car lay in pieces.

And alas for Pierre, no one lived on this side of the mountain. What a long walk back over the mountain it would be, with no friends there to welcome Pierre.

"I shall have to stay here," sighed
Pierre, "but I did so hope
to find a friend."

"If you stay, I shall stay, too,"
bleated Goat.

"And I," baahed Sheep.

"And I," growled Bear.

"That is exactly what my friend would say!" cried Pierre.

"Then I must be your friend," bleated Goat.

"And I," baahed Sheep.

"And I," growled Bear.

"And I must be yours," said Pierre.

Not one friend but three—three friends for Pierre and three friends for Goat, and for Sheep, and for Bear.

And there they lived
on the other side of the mountain.

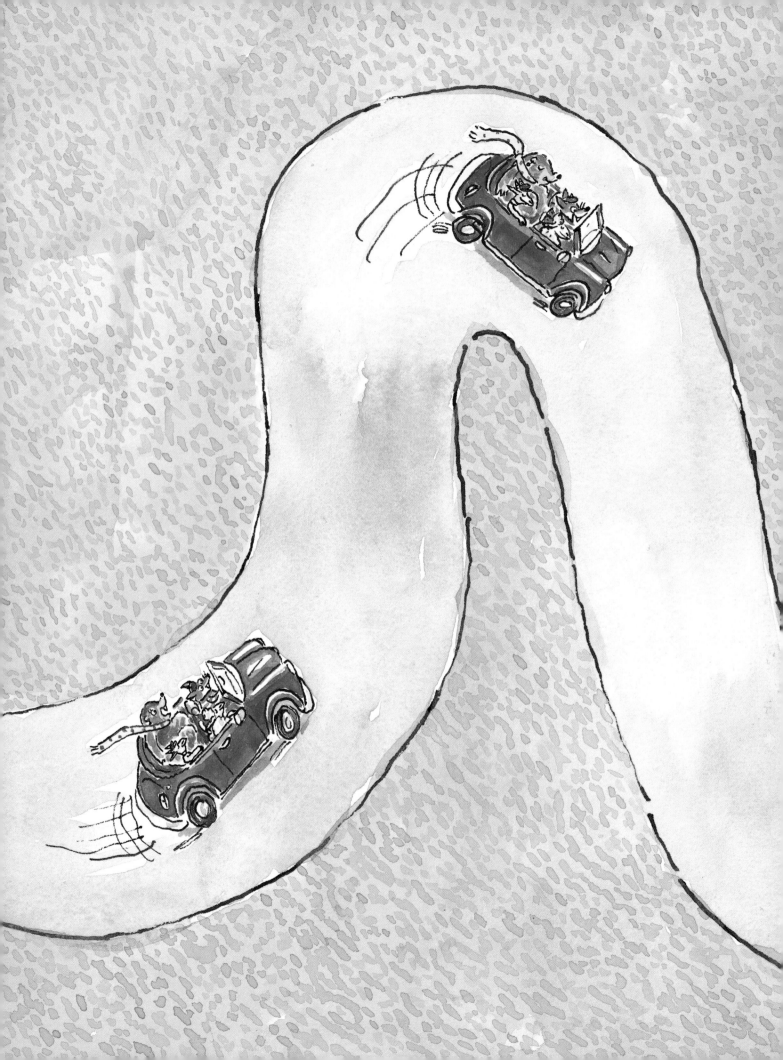